Dear Parents:

Congratulations! Your child is taking the first steps on an exciting journey. The destination? Independent reading!

STEP INTO READING® will help your child get there. The program offers five steps to reading success. Each step includes fun stories and colorful art or photographs. In addition to original fiction and books with favorite characters, there are Step into Reading Non-Fiction Readers, Phonics Readers and Boxed Sets, Sticker Readers, and Comic Readers—a complete literacy program with something to interest every child.

Learning to Read, Step by Step!

Ready to Read **Preschool–Kindergarten**
• big type and easy words • rhyme and rhythm • picture clues
For children who know the alphabet and are eager to begin reading.

Reading with Help **Preschool–Grade 1**
• basic vocabulary • short sentences • simple stories
For children who recognize familiar words and sound out new words with help.

Reading on Your Own **Grades 1–3**
• engaging characters • easy-to-follow plots • popular topics
For children who are ready to read on their own.

Reading Paragraphs **Grades 2–3**
• challenging vocabulary • short paragraphs • exciting stories
For newly independent readers who read simple sentences with confidence.

Ready for Chapters **Grades 2–4**
• chapters • longer paragraphs • full-color art
For children who want to take the plunge into chapter books but still like colorful pictures.

STEP INTO READING® is designed to give every child a successful reading experience. The grade levels are only guides; children will progress through the steps at their own speed, developing confidence in their reading. The F&P Text Level on the back cover serves as another tool to help you choose the right book for your child.

Remember, a lifetime love of reading starts with a single step!

For Rosemary Stimola
—M.M.

To my wizard friend, Mitantsoa.
With love and magic.
—S.C.

Text copyright © 2023 by Michelle Meadows
Cover art and interior illustrations copyright © 2023 by Sawyer Cloud

All rights reserved. Published in the United States by Random House Children's Books, a division of Penguin Random House LLC, New York.

Step into Reading, Random House, and the Random House colophon are registered trademarks of Penguin Random House LLC.

Visit us on the Web!
rhcbooks.com

Educators and librarians, for a variety of teaching tools, visit us at RHTeachersLibrarians.com

Library of Congress Cataloging-in-Publication Data
Names: Meadows, Michelle, author. | Cloud, Sawyer, illustrator.
Title: Maxie Wiz and the magic charms / by Michelle Meadows ; illustrated by Sawyer Cloud.
Description: First edition. | New York : Random House Children's Books, 2023. | Series: Step into reading | Audience: Ages 4–6. | Summary: Maxie embarks on a quest to collect five charms for her magic spell.
Identifiers: LCCN 2022049432 (print) | LCCN 2022049433 (ebook) | ISBN 978-0-593-57136-1 (trade) | ISBN 978-0-593-57137-8 (library binding) | ISBN 978-0-593-57138-5 (ebook)
Subjects: CYAC: Stories in rhyme. | Magic—Fiction. | Charms—Fiction. | LCGFT: Stories in rhyme. | Picture books.
Classification: LCC PZ8.3.M4625 Mc 2023 (print) | LCC PZ8.3.M4625 (ebook) | DDC [E]—dc23

Printed in the United States of America
10 9 8 7 6 5 4 3 2 1

First Edition

This book has been officially leveled by using the F&P Text Level Gradient™ Leveling System.

Maxie Wiz and the Magic Charms

by Michelle Meadows

illustrated by Sawyer Cloud

Random House 🏠 New York

Magic homework.

Time to start.

Maxie Wiz

makes a chart.

Magic charms!

Can you find four?

Bonus point:

find one more!

Find five charms
to cast a spell.

The first charm is
a white seashell.

Maxie Wiz
can pass this test!

Ready for
a magic quest!

White seashell is number one.

Thank you, Mermaid
in the sun.

Golden feather,
number two.

Thank you, Owl.

Hoo hoo hoo!

Silver stone is
number three.

Thank you, Grandma.

So shiny!

17

Unicorn hair,
number four.

Thank you, Fairy.

Snip some more!

Hocus-pocus, serpent snout.

Help this tooth wiggle out.

Sea serpent tooth,
number five.
Thank you, Serpent.
Watch him dive!

Stone, tooth, hair,
feather, shell.

Make a wish
and cast a spell.

Magic charms
in a row.
Hocus-pocus!
Sparkle, glow. . . .

Uh-oh!
No glow!

Nothing happens.
Did she fail?
Dragon hugs her
with its tail.

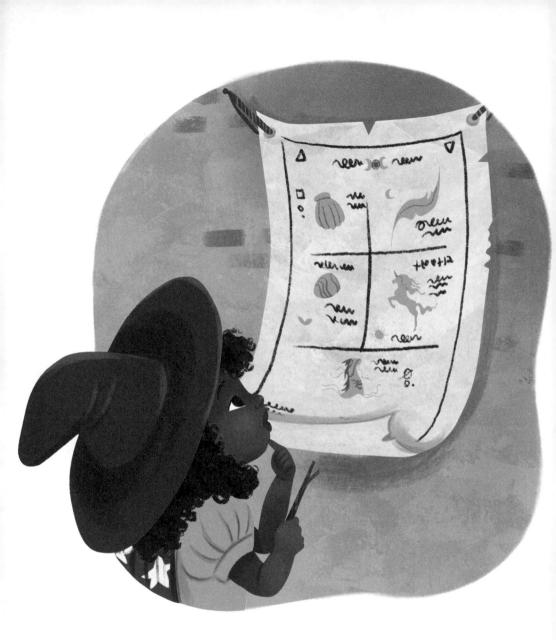

Read the spell,
double-check.

Wear the charms
around your neck.

Hocus-pocus!

Sparkle . . .

WHOA!
Magic charms
make glitter glow!